THIS BOOK BELONGS TO:

_____

To the thousands of little girls who
are my pinkie promise partners. —E. W.

To all kids who want to build
a better, kinder world. —C. C.

Henry Holt and Company, *Publishers since 1866* • Henry Holt® is a registered trademark of Macmillan Publishing Group, LLC. • 120 Broadway, New York, NY 10271 • mackids.com • Text copyright © 2021 by Elizabeth Warren. Illustrations copyright © 2021 by Charlene Chua. All rights reserved. • Our books may be purchased in bulk for promotional, educational, or business use. Please contact your local bookseller or the Macmillan Corporate and Premium Sales Department at (800) 221-7945 ext. 5442 or by email at MacmillanSpecialMarkets@macmillan.com. Library of Congress Cataloging-in-Publication Data is available. • First Edition, 2021 • Book design by Jen Keenan. • Printed in the United States of America by Phoenix Color, Hagerstown, Maryland. • The art for this book was created in Photoshop, using a PC and a Wacom Cintiq tablet. ISBN 978-1-250-80102-9 • 10 9 8 7 6 5 4 3 2

PINKIE PROMISES

ELIZABETH WARREN

•ILLUSTRATED BY CHARLENE CHUA•

GODWINBOOKS

Henry Holt and Company • New York

Polly was tired of hearing what girls can't do.

When she offered to help Uncle Ed fix a leak, Uncle Ed said, "That's *NOT* what girls do."

When she decided to build a drawbridge for her school project, her brother Jack said, "That's *NOT* what girls do."

When she started to wash the car, her neighbor
Mr. Lee said, "That's *NOT* what girls do."

Polly's mother said, "I have an idea.
There's a giant rally in town."

"We can go see someone who is running for president."

The rally was big and noisy, and lots of people cheered.
At the end, Polly and her mother went up front.

The woman smiled at Polly. "My name is
Elizabeth. I'm running for president."

"You are?"
"Yes. I want to lead our country."

"THAT'S WHAT GIRLS DO!"

And they made a pinkie promise to remember.

Monday was Polly's first day at a new school.

Polly saw lots of boys and girls.
She didn't know anyone.

"I know this is all new.
Can you do this?" her mother asked.

Polly stood straight and said, "Yes, I can be brave. Because THAT'S WHAT GIRLS DO."

She gave her mother a pinkie promise
and walked in the front door.

The next afternoon, Polly had a soccer game.

The game was tied, and each side got one more kick to score.
The coach turned to Polly. "I know everyone is watching.
Can you do this?"

Polly stood straight and said, "Yes, I can be strong. Because THAT'S WHAT GIRLS DO." She gave her coach a pinkie promise and walked onto the field.

On Saturday, Polly and Bailey were headed to the dog park when they saw a boy crying. He said his dog was lost, and he was afraid.

No one else was around. The boy asked, "Can you help me?"

Polly stood straight and said, "Yes, I can help. Because THAT'S WHAT GIRLS DO." She gave the boy a pinkie promise, and they worked out a plan to find the missing dog.

The next week, Polly's teacher said they would elect a class president, someone to lead when they lined up to go outside. Polly thought she would be a good president, so she raised her hand to run.

When the time came for speeches,
a classmate asked if she would
make a good president.

Polly stood straight and said, "Yes, I can be a leader. Because THAT'S WHAT GIRLS DO."

And she held up her hand for a pinkie promise with everyone.

That night Polly's mother read her
a story and tucked her in. As she
leaned over to kiss her, she whispered
in Polly's ear, "Dream big."

Polly smiled. "Yes, I will dream big.
BECAUSE THAT'S WHAT GIRLS DO."
And they made a pinkie promise to remember.

Then Polly snuggled down under the covers,
resting up for another day of pinkie promises.